Stargazer to the Sultan

by BARBARA K. WALKER

and MINE SÜMER

illustrated by JOSEPH LOW

Parents' Magazine Press
NEW YORK: 1967

Other books by Barbara Walker

Just Say Hic!
Hilili and Dilili
Watermelons, Walnuts and the
Wisdom of Allah

To Selcuk Sümer and Terri Sue

Once there was and once there wasn't, when yesterday was today and the sieve lay in the hay—well, in those times there was an old woodcutter who lived at the edge of a village. Every day he trudged off to the forest, a stout rope and an axe over one shoulder and a bit of bread and cheese in a string bag over the other. In the morning, *chut-chut-chut*, he chopped, and in the afternoon, "Wood! Wood! Wood!" he cried, selling his bundle in the marketplace. Allah willing, the woodcutter earned a few *kurus,* enough to buy for himself and his wife a loaf of bread, an onion, a cutting of cheese, and three or five olives.

Life would have rolled on year after year in this manner if his wife had been content. But, alas, she dreamed only of being rich. As fate would have it, she was passing the *hamam* one day with her water pitcher when a handsome litter, carried by four servants, arrived before the bathhouse. Out stepped a woman with a dress so beautiful and gems so glittering that the woodcutter's wife could scarcely trust her own senses. She watched as three servants followed the woman into the bath, carrying her parcels of towels and sweetmeats and elegant clean clothing.

As soon as the bathhouse door had closed behind them, the woodcutter's wife tugged at the sleeve of the *hamam* keeper. "Who *is* she?" she whispered.

"Oh, don't you know?" he exclaimed. "She is the wife of the sultan's chief stargazer."

"A stargazer," she mused as she filled her pitcher at the village fountain. "My husband, too, must become a stargazer to the sultan. Then *I* shall go here and there in beautiful gowns and jingle with jewels and have servants to follow me, bearing my bundles."

From the moment her husband entered the cottage that evening, he heard little but stargazer, stargazer. "You must become a stargazer to the sultan," the woman insisted, with her husband all the while staring at her as if she had mislaid her wits. "Surely you want me to live in a beautiful house and have fine dresses and wear jewels at my throat. Look! Just *look* at these patches on patches I am wearing!"

Finally she stopped for a moment to catch her breath. "My wife," said the woodcutter patiently, "how am I to become a stargazer to the sultan? Of *course* I should like to have you live in a beautiful house and to own all the lovely things that women long for. But I am such a poor grasshopper of a man that I can barely keep us in bread and cheese. Who would even *dream* that I could become a stargazer? Pray, wife, be content with what is at hand. After all,

we have our own cottage, and enough to eat, and clothing for our backs."

But, indeed, who could make such a woman listen to reason? She kept after the poor man and *after* him, with the woodcutter all the while saying, "Oh, my dear, how can I? How can you ask such a thing of me?" At length, being a goodhearted man and fond of his wife, he agreed at least to think about the matter.

A few days later, the woodcutter's wife was wakened by the voice of the town crier, shouting street by street and alleyway by alleyway, "Lost! Lost! The sultan's daughter has lost her most valuable ring. Reward! Reward! The sultan offers a handsome reward for the finder of the ring."

"Get up! Get up, my husband!" called the woodcutter's wife. "Here is the chance we have been seeking. Go at once to the sultan and tell him you are an astrologer of special power and can find the ring belonging to his daughter. If you are successful, we can lead a rich and full life. Go. And do not come back into this house until you have become a stargazer to the sultan."

Many years of his wife's nimble tongue had been sample enough to tell the woodcutter that here he faced a road which had no turning. "I begin with the name of Allah," he murmured, and, trembling from nose to toes, he put one foot before the other until he had arrived at the sultan's gate. There he announced himself as a new astrologer, come to find the missing ring. Immediately, he was led into the presence of the sultan himself. "Understand, astrologer, that if you find the ring you will be richly rewarded. If you *fail,* the loss of your head must pay the price of your bad judgment," the sultan declared, marveling that this mere mite of a man could possess such remarkable powers.

"Ah, sire, I *do* understand," the woodcutter answered. "I have but one request, if you will be pleased to grant it."

"Yes, yes? And what is that?"

"I must be left alone for forty days and forty nights, forty nights in which to study Allah's handiwork in the stars and forty days in which to deliberate upon His mercies. At the end of that time, Allah willing, the truth will be revealed." The little woodcutter knew all too well the only truth that could be known at the close of his watching and waiting: that his claim had been beyond his power to fulfill.

The sultan pondered. Then, "Since my own astrologers—even my chief stargazer—have been unable to promise as much, you may *have* your forty days and forty nights," the sultan agreed. Calling his most trusted servant, the ruler had the woodcutter taken to a room with one wide window near the ceiling. The key was turned in the lock, and the poor woodcutter was left alone with his thoughts.

Day after day he paced the flagstone floor; night after night he watched the endless procession of the stars. But what truth could *stars* tell a simple woodcutter except that he was indeed no astrologer at all?

Long as he might look at the stars, his gazing would discover no ring. It would serve only to remind him of the insignificance of such a grasshopper as he in the eyes of Allah.

Each day the sultan's favorite servant came to bring food to the woodcutter. Wonderful food it was, too, straight from the sultan's table. But in the face of such a fate as his, the woodcutter had no stomach for food. For him, these fine meals brought but a single comfort: a certain way of counting the passing of the days until the sultan must learn the truth which now rested heavily on the heart of the new astrologer. Each evening, just before the servant came to carry away the tray, the poor woodcutter removed one small plate and added it to the pile growing all too quickly in the corner of the room, each time murmuring to himself, "Thirty more days, and then the sultan will know," or "Twenty-nine more days, and then the sultan will know."

Now, in fact, a great fear had been growing in the heart of the servant, for it was he himself who had stolen the ring belonging to the sultan's daughter. Coming and going, he had one day seen his opportunity and, trusting he would remain unsuspected, he had slipped the ring into the lining of his sleeve. As the time for the stargazer's deliberations drew to a close, the servant chanced to overhear the new astrologer murmuring, "Three more days, and then the sultan will know." Certain that his secret had been discovered, he decided that the only hope for his desperate case rested in the hands of the little stargazer, clearly a kindhearted man despite his remarkable wisdom.

The next evening, instead of merely handing the tray inside, the servant carried it into the room and set it down in its place upon the floor. Then, closing the door and locking it from the inside, he sank to his knees before the dumfounded woodcutter. "Please, sire," he begged, "listen to my story, the tale of a wretched man indeed. Then, if Allah moves your heart to do so, help me!"

With his eyes flowing like two fountains in his anxiety and grief, he poured forth the account of his theft, sparing not a single detail. "You said last evening, 'Only three more days, and then the sultan will know,'" he concluded. "Now there are only *two* days left before the truth will be revealed. Allah be praised, you, good sire, will never feel the pain one heedless act can bring. How can you, at once a wise and innocent man, know the torment of sleepless nights and the anguish of joyless days that have been mine? But, sire, you *do* know this: if the sultan learns of my guilt, I shall lose not only my bread and my bed, but my head! Please, sire, have pity upon me. Do not tell the sultan of my misdeed. I shall do any- thing—*anything*—if only you will save me from the fate that lies in store for me when the truth becomes known."

For the first time in thirty-eight days, the little woodcutter drew a comfortable breath. Allah alone had spared him, this small grasshopper of a man;

therefore, could he himself fail to pity the trembling one still kneeling before him? Grasping the servant by the hands, he gazed into his eyes. "Fear not. Allah willing, I shall take care of the matter in such a fashion that the sultan will never know who stole the ring. The *truth* will not be known, but the ring will be found. There is one thing, and one thing only, that you must do. On the morrow, buy in the marketplace a pure black cock, one with not a single fleck or feather lighter than midnight. While the other household

servants are still at prayer, add this cock to the flock in the sultan's poultry yard. On the fortieth day, force the black cock to swallow a bit of dough containing the ring. Then leave the rest to me. If you do exactly as I have said, I shall not reveal your secret to the sultan."

Earnestly promising to do as the woodcutter had directed, the grateful servant arose, unlocked the door, and left the room. As for the woodcutter, suddenly he had found his appetite, and he ate all the foods brought from the sultan's table, his heart each moment singing with relief and joy.

Very early on the morning of the forty-first day, the sultan ordered the servant to lead the new astrologer into his presence. Assured that all had been made ready, the woodcutter walked confidently into the room where the sultan awaited him.

"Well, you have had the forty days and forty nights which you requested," the sultan began. "Now, where is the ring?"

"I shall show you the ring in the courtyard today before the call for noontime prayers," the woodcutter answered. "Meanwhile, please summon to appear before you just inside the courtyard gate every person in your household, of whatever rank, from the highest official to the lowliest servant. In addition, cause to be brought to the gate every animal belonging to you and within your palace grounds—dogs, cats, horses, cattle, poultry—all living creatures, that they may pass in procession before you. Allah willing, the ring will be revealed."

Curious indeed to discover how the woodcutter would detect the thief, the sultan sent criers to summon his entire household. First in procession came the women, from the highest to the lowest, from those richly attired to those in patches, all heavily veiled. Not a word of accusation passed the lips of the new astrologer, and the women returned to their own quarters in the harem and elsewhere about their business.

Next, beginning with the grand vizir, came the officials, splendidly dressed. These were closely followed by all the male servants whose work lay within the confines of the palace wall. Making proper obeisance before the ruler, they passed in solemn, silent procession. Still no sign of accusation came from the stargazer, and the men left the presence of the sultan, to engage in whispered wonderings about the guilty one.

At last came the animals, one by one, some mute and some in protest against this strange turn of affairs. Suddenly the astrologer spoke. "Sire, yonder struts a black cock. Have him seized and killed. Within his crop you will find the ring you seek."

Immediately, the cock was caught and carried to the sultan. It was but the matter of a moment to relieve the cock at once of his breath and of his burden. Just as the woodcutter had declared, within the crop gleamed the ring belonging to the sultan's daughter.

Turning to the woodcutter, the sultan announced, "You must now have the reward you so justly deserve for your services. I pronounce you an official stargazer to the sultan. As soon as you wish, you may move with your household into the small palace just outside my gate. There you will lead a rich and full life."

The dazed woodcutter, after taking proper leave of the sultan, hurried home to tell his wife the outcome of his labors. Since the two had little or nothing of value to carry with them, they readied themselves in no time at all to enter the splendid home that was now theirs. Day after day, the wife preened herself before her mirror, trying on one new dress after another, and feasting her eyes upon the gems given to her at the sultan's command. Servants scurried here and there, and none could be prouder than the woodcutter's wife as she sent them about their business. What could be more to her taste than such a life as this?

As for the little woodcutter, day after day he sat in idleness, his brain a-scramble and his throat a-tip-tap with anxiety, for who could tell what service might next be required of him by the sultan? The more accustomed his wife became to their new life, the less comfortable the old woodcutter felt. All too soon, these things could be snatched away, and what pleasure could such borrowed splendor bring an honest heart?

One day as the woodcutter sat meditating alone in their garden, his wife ran to him in great agitation. "My dear," she cried, "you must *do* something. I cannot go on any longer in this poor fashion!"

Staring at his wife, the woodcutter replied, "*What* poor fashion? It seems to me that we are living in very *fine* fashion. A short time ago, we praised Allah daily for the meager life we shared in our cottage. Surely we should be even more grateful for this elegant home in which we dwell. Just see how lovely you look in your new gowns. And note the glitter of gold at your throat. How can you call *this* poor fashion?"

"Ah," she sighed, "until today I felt fortunate. But this morning I discovered that the *chief* stargazer to the sultan has a kiosk within the palace wall itself. His wife wears dresses far more beautiful than mine, and her gems make mine look paltry indeed. I am no longer satisfied, my dear. You must become the sultan's chief stargazer. Then I shall be happy."

"Oh, my wife, let not your heart be troubled by envy," he urged. "Such luxury is not needful for us. Please be content with what we have."

But it is easier to make a camel jump a ditch than to make a fool listen to reason. The wife would not accept anything less than the life offered in that kiosk within the palace wall. "Go," she said. "And do not expect a meal under this roof until you have become chief stargazer to the sultan."

Head in hands, the little woodcutter considered his dilemma. Being a sensible man, he valued his life far more than an elegant roof above his head. This house they had was quite fine enough for him, and in time his wife must learn to accept it as the best that he could give her. Well he knew the risk of further venture as a stargazer. Far from wishing to become chief stargazer to the sultan, the humble woodcutter desired freedom from even his present official post. As long as he must dwell in dread, no roof could truly shelter him, be it humble or fine.

Suddenly he was struck by a plan at once so simple and so sound that he resolved to act upon it. Since the sultan considered his astrologers beyond question men of wisdom, one who appeared the most fantastic of fools could scarcely be thought worthy of such a title. The new astrologer must merely behave as one who had entirely lost his wits, so that he could no longer be relied on as an astrologer. Relieved of his position, he could then truly enjoy the comfortable life which his first venture had miraculously brought him.

Waiting that afternoon until the palace courtyard had ceased to buzz with its midday activity, he tucked up his robe, set his turban askew, and rushed about here and there within the palace grounds, shouting, "The sultan! The sultan! Who has seen the sultan? Quickly! Quickly! Something must be done at *once*."

Officials and servants ran toward him from all directions. "*Hush*, man. Are you mad? What are you doing, shouting thus when the household is at rest? What can you be *thinking* of?"

But the woodcutter refused to answer their questions, crying again and again, "The sultan! Where *is* he?"

At last a servant reported that the sultan was in the bath and must not be disturbed.

"Disturbed, eh!" shouted the woodcutter. "He will be disturbed indeed when the roof of his *hamam* tumbles in upon his head! I *must* see the sultan at once."

Immediately, the new astrologer was seized by two of the sultan's bodyguard. "The man has surely taken leave of his senses," one declared. "There is not a stouter roof in the whole kingdom than the dome above the sultan's *hamam*!" And they struggled to lead the distraught woodcutter away.

Meanwhile, above the music and splashing of the bath the sultan had heard the crazed shouting in the hall, and, hastily wrapping himself in a large towel, he emerged into the corridor to confront the culprit. No sooner had the last of his towel trailed through the doorway when with a thundering crash the roof of the *hamam* fell in, leaving the bath a ruin.

Weak with shock and disbelief, the sultan staggered against his new astrologer, who was of all men the most amazed at the sudden crumbling of the dome. "Ah, my stargazer," babbled the sultan, "no man of ordinary powers could have foreseen such a calamity. By your wisdom you have saved my life. For this singular service, I pronounce you chief stargazer to the sultan."

Amazed at the outcome of his plan, the woodcutter went home to tell his wife what had happened. She was almost delirious with delight, and hastily gathered together the things she considered light in weight but heavy in value. As for the rest, they could be left behind. For would the two not have far more elegant quarters within the wall of the sultan's own palace?

There a splendid kiosk awaited them, with far more servants, and enough dresses and diamonds to gratify even the most demanding of women. In short, the woodcutter's wife was at last satisfied.

Alas for the woodcutter, however, as the complaints of his wife were swallowed up in her content, the demands of the sultan grew in number. Oh, the anxious little astrologer had been asked no further questions. But as chief stargazer, he was expected to be at all times in the sultan's presence—at the sultan's meals, during his rides throughout the countryside, even on his strolls through the palace gardens. Another man might have relished such opportunities, might have basked in such glories, but the heart of the little woodcutter was not as that of other men. For himself he would never have sought such dizzying heights. Well he knew that a single misstep could plunge him into the direst of misfortunes. The slender legs of such a grasshopper as he were not meant to carry him to this high post. One day, he was certain, all would be lost. Thus he sat silent throughout the grand dinners, and mused while others made much of their nearness to the sultan.

Noting this, the sultan thought one day to tease his chief stargazer out of his thoughts. As they strolled down the garden paths that evening, suddenly the sultan reached out and scooped up something into his hand. Holding his closed hand before the astrologer, he said, "You have remarkable powers, indeed. Before all these members of my court I shall prove your powers. Within my hand I hold a small something. If you can tell me what it is, I shall grant whatever you wish. It is within my power to give you what you ask. Is it within your power to tell me what I hold thus helpless within my hand?"

Here was the moment the woodcutter had been dreading. And he had no answer ready. Whatever the sultan had scooped up out of the garden, he held within his hand the life of a poor little grasshopper of a man, stargazer only by strange leaps of fortune.

In despair, the old woodcutter responded with a village proverb: "You jump once, grasshopper, and you survive. You jump twice, grasshopper, and still you live. But the third time you jump, you are caught." Having spoken, he waited before the sultan. He had offered in a proverb the truth of his own life, and beyond it he knew no truth at all.

The sultan, opening his hand, revealed—a grasshopper. "You see?" he said, turning to his courtiers. "Here is a man with remarkable powers indeed, powers beyond those of ordinary men, powers that lie in the spangled heavens above. Now, my chief stargazer, ask what you will, and it shall be granted."

His heart light, his soul filled with relief and joy, the woodcutter answered, "Allah be praised, I have been able to serve your needs, my sultan. What I wish is simply this: I should like no longer to be your stargazer. I want merely to live comfortably and to meditate upon the mercies of Allah."

"Your wish will be granted," the sultan declared. "The kiosk within my palace wall is yours. And you may come and go within my kingdom as you will. But I relieve you at this hour of your title as stargazer to the sultan. Go in peace, and may your way be open."

Thus it was that the little woodcutter was enabled to dwell happily with his wife within the wall of the sultan's palace, with stomach for his food, and with eyes always for the stars, those endless reminders of the care of Allah for even one small grasshopper of a man.

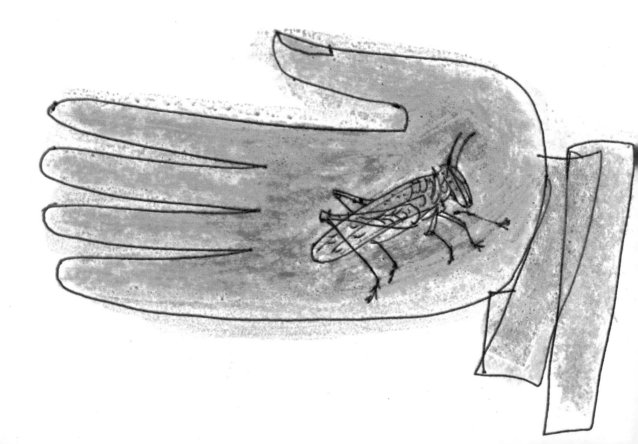